# This book belongs to:

. . . . . . . . . . . . . . . . . . . . . . . . . . . . . . . . . .

. . . . . . . . . . . . . . . . . . . . . . . . . . . . . . . . . .

Retold by Monica Hughes
Illustrated by Gwyneth Williamson

Reading consultants: Betty Root and Monica Hughes

This edition published by Parragon in 2010

Parragon
Queen Street House
4 Queen Street
Bath BA1 1HE, UK

ISBN 978-1-4454-1210-8

Printed in China

# Beauty
## and the
# Beast

Bath · New York · Singapore · Hong Kong · Cologne · Delhi · Melbourne

*Helping your child to read*

These books are closely linked to recognized learning strategies. Their vocabulary has been carefully selected from the word lists recommended by educational experts.

*Read the story*
Read the story
to your child
a few times.

When Beauty got to the castle she went inside.
There was no one inside.
But it was warm and cozy.
And there was food to eat.

Every evening the ugly Beast appeared.
He was good and kind to Beauty.
Beauty grew to like the Beast.

20

*Follow your finger*
Run your finger under
the text as you read.
Your child will soon begin to
follow the words with you.

*Look at the pictures*
Talk about the pictures. They will
help your child to understand the story.

Beauty grew to like the Beast. 21

*Give it a try*
Let your child
try reading the
large type on each
right-hand page.
It repeats a line
from the story.

*Join in*
When your child is ready, encourage
him or her to join in with the main
story text. Shared reading is the first
step to reading alone.

Once upon a time there was a girl called Beauty.
She lived with her father and two greedy sisters.
Beauty was kind and good.

Beauty was kind and good.

One day her father was going to town.
"I will bring you each a gift," he said.
"I want a new dress," said the first sister.
"I want a new hat," said the second sister.
"I would like a red rose," said Beauty.

"I would like a red rose,"
said Beauty.

12

Soon the father was lost.

The father went inside.
There was no one inside.
But it was warm and cozy.
And there was food to eat.

In the morning the father set out
home again.
There was a rose bush in the castle garden.
The father thought of Beauty's gift.
So he picked one red rose.

He picked one red rose.

Suddenly there was a terrible roar.
An ugly beast appeared.
"Why have you stolen my rose?" said
the Beast.
"The red rose is for my daughter,"
said the father.
"Take the rose," said the Beast.
"But you must give me your daughter
in return, or you will die."

"Why have you stolen my rose?" said the Beast.

The father went home.
He told his daughters about the ugly Beast.
"I will go to the Beast," said Beauty.

"I will go to the Beast," said Beauty.

When Beauty got to the castle she
went inside.
There was no one inside.
But it was warm and cozy.
And there was food to eat.

Every evening the ugly Beast appeared.
He was good and kind to Beauty.
Beauty grew to like the Beast.

Beauty grew to like the Beast.

One evening the Beast gave Beauty a
magic mirror.
Beauty looked in the mirror.
She saw her father was sick.
"I must go to my father," said Beauty.
"Promise me you will come back after
three nights," said the Beast.

Beauty went home.
She looked after her father.
After three nights he was better.
But she forgot her promise to the Beast.

Beauty went home.

One day Beauty looked in the magic mirror.
She saw that the Beast was sick.
Then she remembered her promise.
"I must go back to the Beast," said Beauty.

She went back to the castle.
The Beast lay beside the red rose bush.
"Please do not die, Beast," said Beauty.
"I love you."

"I must go back to the Beast."

As if by magic, the Beast changed into
a handsome prince.
"I was under a magic spell," said the prince.
"But your kind words broke the spell."

Soon after, Beauty and the prince were
married, and they lived happily ever after.

The Beast changed into a
handsome prince.

# Look back in your book.
## Can you read these words?

Beauty

Beast

rose

father

sisters

# Can you answer these questions?

What gift did
Beauty want?

Who went to live
with the Beast?

What happened
to the Beast?

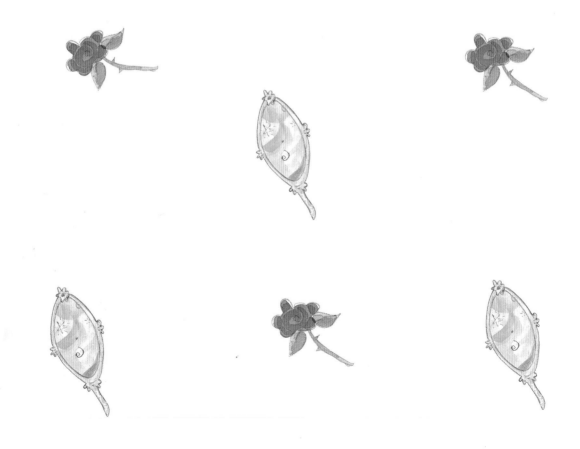